TWISTED SURPRISE

A TWISTED FATE CHRISTMAS NOVELLA

EMERY JACOBS

To Jeanette —

♡ Emery Jacobs xo

Editing & Proofreading:

Dawn Alexander, Evident Ink

Editing by C. Marie

Hot Tree Editing

Julie Deaton, Deaton Author Services

Formatting:

Drue Hoffman, Buoni Amici Press

Cover Design:

Amy Queau, Q Design

Photography:

Max Ellis

Model:

Drew Truckle

AUTHOR'S NOTE

Twisted Surprise is not a stand-alone novella. Twisted Fate must be read first to fully understand this story.

UNTITLED

Life is full of surprises.

~ John Major

1

JOVIE

Four days before Thanksgiving

"I can't go to Georgia with you for Thanksgiving." The words fall from Jack's mouth without warning.

My heart sinks deep into my chest as I stop packing and look over my shoulder at him standing in the doorway of our bedroom. His back is resting against the doorjamb, and his arms are folded across his chest. His face is completely devoid of emotion, not giving me any idea of what's going on.

"Thanksgiving is in four days, Jack. We're supposed to be leaving in the morning," I remind him with a twinge of disappointment in my voice. After three years together, he's only been back home with me a handful of times. It has nothing to do with my parents; they have grown to love him over the years, despite everything that happened with my sister, Piper.

He pushes off the doorframe and makes his way over to me. "I'm sorry about the short notice, but Stone had to head out today because his grandfather's sick, and he needs me at the shop." Jack takes the blouse I'm holding from my hand and places it into the suitcase.

My pulse quickens a bit as a flash of anger rushes through me. Over the last few weeks, Stone has been taking advantage of Jack's generosity with helping out at Southern Stain. I hate to be a bitch about it since his grandfather is sick, but damn, I'm tired of my boyfriend picking up his boss's slack, especially when Jack is not the only tattoo artist employed there.

"Can't someone else fill in?" I huff out the question on an irritated breath. "What about Annie or Fish? Surely one of them would help out since everybody knows we've been planning this trip for months. Plus, I really don't like you spending the holiday alone." Ever since our first Christmas and New Year's together, we've never been apart during a major holiday. In the beginning of our relationship, Jack didn't do very well during the holidays. He would completely shut down because of his past. Now, he's so much better than he used to be, but even at that, it still doesn't change my mind because I don't want to chance him regressing back to the awful place he used to go.

"Jovie, baby, I know what you're thinking." He leans down and kisses my forehead before gently tucking a stray piece of hair behind my ear. "Please don't worry about me. I promise I can handle being alone for a few days. My life is completely different than it was before. We have a life together, you and me." He motions between the two of us. "You make me so fucking happy every single day that my past stays in the past—my mind never goes there."

He cups my face and covers my mouth with his. He's done with this discussion because I'm getting upset. This is what Jack does—always protecting me and my feelings. He redirects the conversation to light touches, sweet kisses, and soft whispers about promises of much more. I'll give it to him—he's really good at diverting my attention. It usually works, but tonight I need to be strong and make sure he fully understands the way I feel.

He kisses me slow and gently, just the way I like it, but it still doesn't excuse the fact that he's sending me to my parents to spend Thanksgiving without him. "It's a holiday, and I want to be with you," I say as I pull my lips away from his. I realize I sound like a whiny child or maybe a spoiled brat, but I'm okay with that because I know that all the whining in the world is probably not going to change the circumstances.

Jack looks down into my eyes and smiles. "Jovie, babe, I love you, and it's killing me not to be with you over the holiday, but I don't have a choice. Southern Stain is Stone's business, and he's my boss. So, if he says I have to keep the shop open during Thanksgiving, then that's what I'll do." He kisses the tip of my nose before dropping his hands from my face.

My chest aches as I hurriedly toss the rest of my things into the case. The irritation I felt a few minutes ago has morphed into sadness. Now, I'm so upset about Jack's absence during the holiday that I don't even care if my clothes are wrinkled or not. Truthfully, I don't want to go anymore. I'd rather stay here and spend Thanksgiving at Southern Stain with him. I blow out a deep breath and close my eyes for a beat. I have to go to my parents—I don't have a choice. My mother has been an alcoholic my entire life. After my sister died, she stopped drinking for a long time, but then about a year ago she started again. According to my dad, she's been doing better recently. Going to meetings, spending time with her sponsor, and she's even doing an outpatient rehab. I'm so proud of her accomplishments—she just recently hit three months of sobriety, and right now she needs me more than I need to stay here. *I'm being ridiculous. It's only five days.*

I open my eyes and tilt my head back, looking up at Jack. "I really don't like him," I deadpan.

"Who?" Jack shoves his hands into the front pockets of his jeans, takes a step back, and smirks.

He knows exactly who I'm talking about. Not only is Stone a male whore who's slept with almost every one of my single friends, a fact that makes it awkward to hang out with him, he's also a jerk for making Jack stay in town and work after he already promised him the time off.

"Please don't tease me, Jack. You know I'm talking about Stone. And you also know how I feel about him."

"Who's teasing? I had no idea you didn't like him." He smirks again.

"Stop it with the lopsided grin. I mean it." He knows exactly how to get to me, and the look he's sporting right now makes me shift my focus from him staying here alone for Thanksgiving to how good he looks when he's wearing nothing but that smirk. "You know when you look at me like that it makes me want to do terribly bad things to you, right?" I say softly as my pulse races.

He moves his mouth closer to me before his lips skim over my cheek, only stopping when he reaches my ear. "What kinds of terribly bad things do you have in mind?" he whispers, his breath warming my skin yet creating a trail of goose bumps at the same time.

"I'll start here," I mutter softly, reaching for the waistband of his jeans before lifting to my toes and kissing his neck. God, I love this guy. Not only is he hot and super sexy, he's sweet and kind and loves me beyond what I could've ever imagined. Even though we had a rough start—and I mean very rough—we've been able to work through his past and somewhat tame my demons.

My fingers work quickly as I unbutton his pants. "Then I'll... I'll...," I stutter, trying to hold back a giggle. "Rip off every piece of clothing you have on before having my way with you." I smile, and the giggle I was holding back escapes in full force.

His gaze drops to mine before he gives me a full-face grin. "Do you really think you're strong enough to complete that task, Ms. Blake?" he questions in a low, husky tone.

"Absolutely," I murmur as I debate whether or not I should shove his jeans and boxers to the floor, climb him like a tree, and ride him until he's begging me to stop. I close my eyes for a brief second before exhaling a long sigh of regret because I can't do all the things I want to do right now. I need to finish our conversation, and he needs to understand that his sexy smirks and flirty antics will not sway me from having this discussion.

I let go of his jeans, open my eyes, and take a step away from him. Then I glance up at his face and give him my best half smile. "I'm sorry I've made such a big deal about you not being able to go. I do understand your job is important and sometimes it has to come first."

He chuckles lightly and steps toward me, grabbing my waist and pulling me flush against his body. "You're forgiven. Now take your clothes off so I can give you a send-off you won't forget." He nuzzles his face against my neck before kissing me just below my ear, firing off tingles throughout my body.

"But I still think you need to talk to Stone about it," I whisper as he continues to nibble on my neck. Dammit, he's making this so difficult.

"Come on, baby, let it go. Talking to Stone about it won't change anything. I'm still gonna have to work." He moves his mouth across my cheek and over my jaw. "Just relax and let me make you feel good." His warm breath skates across my skin, tempting me to give in to him.

"Jack," I whimper.

"Yeah, babe." His voice vibrates against my body as he alternates between licking and biting his way down my neck.

He knows I can't carry on a conversation with him when his mouth is on me. The stubborn part of me wants to pull away and make him talk this out, but the needy part wants to say, "Fuck it," and give in to his touch.

I blow out a long, slow sigh and drop my head back, giving him better access. "Fuck it." I let go and give in. Jack's deep laughter hums against my skin. He knows what he's done. He's getting his way, and his laughter is that of happiness.

My hands quickly skim the hem of his T-shirt before lifting it over his chest. I'm not quite tall enough to push it over his head, and I'm nowhere near strong enough to rip it to shreds. Thankfully Jack knows this, so he yanks it off and tosses it across the room. He frees his body of his jeans, leaving them pooled around his ankles.

I immediately rise to my toes, dragging my lips down his neck and over his hard chest. My movements are slow and determined as my mouth hovers over his right nipple and then moves to his left. He breathes out a heavy moan as he steps out of his jeans and kicks them to the side. My gaze travels to his feet, slides up his strong, muscular legs, and lands on the only stitch of clothing he still has on: boxer briefs that fit him snugly in all the right places, or maybe just in the one place I can't seem to look away from.

My fingers itch to go there, but Jack distracts me for a moment by gently touching my chin and tilting my head back until my focus moves to his face.

"I'm going to miss you." I suck on my bottom lip for a beat while taking in his beautiful face.

Dark brown eyes watch me as I wait for his response. "Then don't go. Stay," he whispers with a shaky voice, his gaze never leaving mine.

"I have to go." I barely get the words out before his mouth crashes over mine. My heart does a little happy dance inside my chest because he asked me to stay.

A deep moan escapes his throat when his kiss becomes hard and urgent. I love hard. Oh, God, how I love hard. And urgent definitely serves a purpose, but not tonight. Tonight, I want slow, steady, and gentle.

"Jack, please slow down. I want this to last... *forever.*" I almost don't get the last word out as I pull away from our kiss and glance up at his face.

"Don't ask me to do that, babe. You know I can't," he whispers only seconds before he presses his lips back to mine. "But for you—" He hesitates a second. "—I always try."

Jack's hands move to my blouse, and he quickly unfastens each button until he's helping me shimmy out of it. He then unhooks my bra quickly before slinging it somewhere behind him. I honestly don't think this man knows what the definition of slow is. But, with each touch, each kiss, I don't care what he does as long as he keeps his word. *Just relax and let me make you feel good.*

He wraps his hands around my waist, lifts me from the floor, and gently tosses me onto the bed.

"The suitcase...." The words aren't even out of my mouth before Jack shoves my case onto the floor, strips his boxer briefs off, climbs onto the mattress, and hovers over me.

"Fuck, you're beautiful," he whispers before reaching underneath my skirt and ripping my panties off.

"Dammit, Jack, that was my favorite pair."

"They're all your favorite pair," he whispers as his lips brush mine.

"If you wouldn't...." My words fade quickly, and the thought of him destroying every pair of panties I own vanishes because now the only thing controlling my mind and my body is his mouth.

He hovers over me, his body lightly touching mine. His lips move to my cheek, my jaw, and then skim down my neck.

A soft moan escapes from somewhere inside of me just before I inhale deeply, breathing in everything that is Jack Alexander. God, he smells so good, fresh and clean like he just took a shower. His scent is so distinctive and so damn sexy.

He lifts his head and looks me in the eye. "What do you want, baby?" His voice is gentle, almost inaudible as his teeth rake over the bare skin of my neck. "Do you want me to fuck you slow, Jovie?" He kisses that sensitive spot just below my ear before whispering, "It'll be fucking hard, but I'll take my time and worship every inch of skin on your hot little body." Jack's lips graze my skin as he moves his mouth back to mine. "Is that what you want me to do, Jovie?" His voice is laced with need.

My breathing is deep and heavy. "Mmmm," I hum as my eyes

flutter closed. His tongue and teeth touch every single inch of my body slowly and methodically until it feels like he's completely devoured me. I release a soft whimper, lifting my hips, pressing my center against his rock-hard cock. A shiver races down my spine and settles in my belly. I tug at my skirt—the last piece of clothing that's keeping me from feeling every inch of his skin against mine.

"This has got to go," I mumble as I lift my bottom and wiggle my hips, moving the skirt down my legs until it falls to the floor. "Fuck me, Jack. I need you to fuck me." My voice is needy. His hands cup my ass, lifting it off the mattress, holding me tight as his erection presses hard at my entrance.

"Damn, Jovie, baby. You feel so good." He grunts softly, pushing himself deep inside me.

I bury my face in the crease of his neck and bite him gently as he shows so much restraint.

I wrap my legs around his waist and lift my hips to meet his every thrust. A sudden tingle shoots through me as Jack scatters kisses to my jaw, moving across to my ear, and finally reaching my neck.

"I don't know how much longer I can do this, baby. Slow is so fucking hard for me." His movements are steady, unhurried, and deliberate. He's giving me exactly what I want, what I need.

Jack's breathing is quick and shallow, and his entire body shakes from restraint. "Slow, so fucking slow…," he breathes out as he pushes deeper inside of me. "You like it slow, don't you, baby?" His question comes out on a long, slow groan.

"Mmmm. Please don't stop." My voice fades into his.

"You don't have to worry about that." He grunts as he thrusts over and over, bringing me closer to breaking apart underneath him. "Come for me, baby." His words are warm on my skin, and my body responds immediately, shaking and quivering from head to toe as I pulse around him. I whisper his name once, twice, three times... my voice growing louder each time.

My body should be wiped out. Spent. But it's not. I'm still wound up so damn tight, wanting more, needing more, so now is the time to let him take what he wants—hard, fast, and greedy.

"Fuck me harder, Jack," I demand.

My words drive him, give him the okay to take what he needs. He thrusts inside of me, pumping forward harder, my body sliding up the bed. My hips rock and my body shudders in response to his movement. Jack's hands settle on my waist, and his groans grow louder. His cock swells within me before he comes on a long, low grunt. He releases a deep breath and then kisses my forehead. "I love you, baby." His words are soft and sweet, so unlike the man who just fucked me so hard that I hope I'm able to crawl out of bed and walk in the morning.

My eyes never leave him, even after he slides out of me and heads toward the bathroom. Long lines of nothing but muscle and tattoos fill my sight. I'm the luckiest girl in the entire world. The sexy man walking away from our bed naked and sated loves me. "I love you too," I whisper, knowing he can't hear me. Jack vanishes from my sight as the door to the bathroom closes.

I refuse to let us being apart for Thanksgiving ruin my holiday season. We'll be together for Christmas and New Year's. We'll celebrate with our friends, and when we're not celebrating, we'll be spending time in bed making up for the time we lost this week. *That's more like it.* My newfound positive attitude is making me feel better already.

I snatch a hair clasp from the nightstand and throw my frizzy mop into a messy bun on top of my head. I climb out of bed and grab Jack's T-shirt from the floor, bringing it to my nose and inhaling his scent for the last time until I return from my parents' house. God, I'm gonna miss him. *It's only a few days. Don't be so needy.*

I throw his T-shirt on, snag my suitcase from the floor, and toss it onto the bed to finish packing for my trip.

2

JOVIE

Thanksgiving Day

"Are you pregnant?" Mom asks as I turn up my glass of sweet tea. The cold liquid barely hits my throat before my body convulses and tea shoots from my mouth and nose. What the hell is wrong with her? Before I question her rationale for discussing the possibility of me being with child at Thanksgiving dinner, I cut my eyes toward my dad. He immediately looks away, like he's been caught watching the whole thing go down but doesn't want me to know he's actually paying attention to our conversation. *Great.* There's nothing like discussing your sex life at the dinner table in front of your father.

"Why would you even ask me such a question?" I bark out, looking her square in the eye. "Especially right now." I flick my eyes toward my father, who is staring at his plate. My dad, the police chief of Brownsboro, Georgia, is a man of few words. It's the way he looks at me—or in this case, the way he won't look at me—that tells me everything I need to know. He doesn't look very happy, or maybe it's disappointment written across his face. It doesn't really matter because I'm not pregnant, and I don't want him worrying about something that's not even true. I know he's not really happy about me living with Jack, but as long as I'm "living in sin" in Houston and not Brownsboro, he can deal with it. Why? Because it's not right under his nose, so he can put it in a compartment in the very back of his mind and pretend it's not really happening.

"Hmm… you just haven't been yourself since you arrived a couple of days ago." Mom stops eating and forces a small smile on her face. "You've done nothing but lie around all day and stare at your phone. You've hardly eaten anything and have told me repeatedly that you don't feel very well."

"So, me not going out and drinking my weight in alcohol every night with my old high school friends and not binging on pizza and tacos means I'm pregnant?" *Fuck!* I regret the words as soon as they leave my mouth. Mom has had a long, hard road full of drunken nights followed by short periods of sobriety. Every time she's sober for longer than a few days—like now, when she's at the three-month mark—we all get excited that this might be the time she quits for good, but it also means tiptoeing around her like I'm walking on eggshells. I hate it. It's been this way most of my life. The only time she was sober for an extended period of time was after my sister died.

"Jovie!" Dad's deep voice rumbles loudly throughout the dining room.

"Sorry," I whisper as I lower my head. Suddenly I'm no longer hungry. I used to love the holidays, but this year I can't bring myself to even pretend to be happy. I can't even put my finger on the exact reason. It's more like a combination of several things. My mom is fighting to stay sober, my boyfriend isn't here, and my dad is on pins and needles praying we make it through the day without me saying something that causes my mom to have a meltdown and start drinking before Christmas.

"It's okay, honey. Jovie didn't mean anything by what she said. Her hormones are probably all out of sorts, and it's making her a bit cranky," Mom says as she directs her attention toward my dad.

"Mom, I'm not pregnant." I lift my head and look directly at her. "I'm just a little down because Jack had to work, that's all. I'm fine."

"How do you know you're not pregnant? Have you taken a test?" Her voice is hopeful.

Why would she even want me to be pregnant? I'm not married, I still have another semester left before graduating from college, and then I plan on immediately enrolling in graduate school. This is not the time for me to be pregnant.

"No, Mom, I haven't taken a pregnancy test." God, this is so damn awkward, especially since my dad is no longer pissed about my mention of alcohol and has gone back to staring at his plate —pretending he's no longer listening to the conversation.

"Honey, you just have all the signs of being pregnant. That's all I'm saying, and if you are, it's okay. You and Jack have been together for long enough that I'm sure he'll take care of you and the baby."

"If it'll make you feel better, I'll take a pregnancy test in the morning." I think at this point it's best if I just give in. It's Thanksgiving Day; we should be enjoying our meal and each other, not arguing about something as ridiculous as me being pregnant.

"I think that's a great idea. Don't you, Dan?" She looks toward my father.

"Whatever you say, sweetheart." He glances at me before "Thank you" silently falls from his mouth.

I blow out a deep breath and give him a small smile.

"Is Layla coming by tonight?" Mom asks, referring to my best friend. I've always considered Layla as my savior. She was the first person I met when we moved to Brownsboro, Georgia, and from day one, her friendship saved me from the sadness that was forever consuming me in this house. Mom was so depressed after my sister was killed, and Dad was always working. Layla became the only person I could count on, and she's never failed me.

I move the fruit salad around on my plate as I shake my head. "No, she didn't come home for Thanksgiving. She decided to stay in Houston and spend the holiday with her fiancé and his family."

"Fiancé?" Her voice comes out a bit pitchy.

"Yes, her fiancé. I told you Sebastian proposed to her earlier this year." I tap my finger on my chin as I try to remember what month they got engaged. "Hmm... I think it was March or April." I shrug. "I can't remember the exact date, but I told you." I'm sure it was during a time when she was heavily sedated from one too many martinis.

Mom narrows her eyebrows as she begins to think out loud, which is annoying, but I don't say anything. I just let her ramble as I continue to move food around on my plate, thankful that she's moved on to something other than me being pregnant. "How long have they been dating? It seems kind of quick to me. And I wonder why Carla hasn't mentioned it to me." Carla is Layla's mom, and she became friends with my mother soon after Layla and I became close.

I really need to get away from this table and this day, maybe spend some time studying or watching television. I just need a break from the emotional roller coaster of the past couple of days. "Dinner was great, but I'm stuffed," I say to no one in particular.

"No room for dessert?" Mom pushes away from the table and stands just as I grab my plate and head toward the kitchen.

"No. I can't eat another bite," I tell her.

She glances at my plate before her gaze meets mine. The silence that falls between us is awkward, uncomfortable, but I don't force another conversation with her that would more than likely cause more tension.

I move to the opposite end of the table where she is standing. "Thank you for dinner. It was so good." I kiss her cheek before looking back at my father and then heading toward the kitchen to put away my dishes.

"Jovie," Mom calls out as I walk away. Dammit, I almost made it. Only two more steps then I'd be in the kitchen and I could take the back stairs to my room to avoid any more face-to-face time with my parents tonight.

I stop and glance over my shoulder without saying a word. Her eyes are dull, but she's giving me her best attempt at a smile.

"I'm glad you're here. I've really missed you." Her voice is soft and sincere.

Now I feel awful because I haven't been a very good daughter since I've been home. I want to say something, but I'm not really sure what, so I just give her a nod and a small smile before walking away.

3

JOVIE

The day after Thanksgiving

My phone chimes a familiar tune as it vibrates against the granite countertop of the bathroom vanity. I inhale a much-needed deep breath and glance at the screen even though I know exactly who that ringtone belongs to. Jack. I want to cry and beg him to come get me, take me home, and hold me for the rest of the day. Between my mom being extremely overbearing, my dad walking around on edge, and me attempting to study for finals, my nerves are shot to hell. It's a miracle I haven't had a panic attack.

"Hey, I miss you" are the first words I say when I answer his call.

"Hey, baby, I miss you too. Is everything okay?" he asks, his voice laced with concern.

I hesitate a beat as I glance at the pregnancy test lying on the countertop. "Yeah, everything is fine. I'm just ready to come home."

"I'm sorry I didn't have a chance to call you back...." His voice fades as Mom knocks a couple of times on the bathroom door before pushing it open and stepping inside. *I should have locked the damn door.*

"It's been five minutes—have you looked at the test yet? Is it positive?" she blurts out, and I swear her voice echoes throughout the small room. She reaches for it, but I block her before she's able to grab it.

"Mom, please. I'm on the phone. We can do this in a few minutes."

"What's going on? Is that your mom?" Jack's voice is loud and clear.

"Yeah, hang on a second." I scramble to hit the mute button so he doesn't have to hear anything else she says. She's been on a roll, and there's no stopping her until she gets her hands on the pregnancy test.

"Go ahead and take a look," I tell her. I'm doing my best not to sound irritated, but it's hard.

"Let's do it together," she says with a little too much cheerfulness in her voice, or maybe it's hope and not cheer.

I glance in her direction, and she's smiling at me as she shows off both hands with fingers crossed. *You've got to be kidding me.*

I fight the eye roll because it would be wrong. "Okay, but we have to hurry—Jack's still on the phone."

She nods as we peer over the sink at the negative pregnancy test. I breathe out a sigh of relief, even though I'm not sure why because there was never any chance in my mind that it would be anything but negative. I think it's probably because Mom planted that little seed of doubt and, of course, my thoughts just took off with it.

Her smile disappears, and her eyes fill with disappointment. Why do I suddenly feel terrible that I'm not pregnant? "It's just not the right time. I promise one day you'll be a grandmother." My voice is shaky as tears pool in my eyes. My heart is breaking for her. She's lost so much in her life. I just hope this doesn't send her back to the bottle.

She gives me a hug before leaving me alone in the bathroom with sadness and worry for her swirling through my head.

"Did you take a pregnancy test?" Jack's voice rings out loudly from the phone.

Shit. I thought I hit mute, but I guess in my struggle to fight off Mom's grabby hands and echoing voice, I didn't cut Jack off from everything that just went down.

I take in a deep breath and then slowly release it. Jack and I have never had a pregnancy scare. We've never even talked about kids or our future. We just live every day together without worry and without fear. At least that's the way it used to be, but lately I've been questioning every move he makes. *Stop being so insecure —everything is fine.*

He swallows so loudly on the other end of the line I swear I can feel the vibration throughout my entire body. "I thought you were on the pill."

"I am on the pill. It's not what you think." I hesitate a beat so I can figure out how to explain this fucked-up situation to him, but he doesn't give me time.

"How can it not be what I think if you took a pregnancy test? Why didn't you tell me you thought you were pregnant? Dammit, Jovie, we talk about shit like this. I don't understand how you could run off to your parents, thinking you're pregnant without breathing a word about it to me first." *We never talk about shit like this.*

"Please, Jack, just let me explain. You weren't supposed to hear any of this." A couple of tears fall as my attempt not to cry is failing miserably.

"So, you weren't planning to tell me?" His tone is harsh. Even though he's hundreds of miles away, I swear I can see his face. His jaw is clenched, his eyes closed. His neck is probably red, and it's quickly moving up to his face. He rarely ever gets mad, but from the sound of his voice, I think he's about to his boiling point.

"No, I was going to tell you when I got home, but I never thought I was pregnant. It was Mom. It's a long story, and I just can't do this right now, Jack. Just believe me when I tell you this is a huge misunderstanding." I balance the phone between my cheek and shoulder as I wipe the tears from my face.

"I have enough going on right now without having to worry about this," he says, his voice laced with irritation.

What else does he have going on? He hasn't mentioned anything to me except working during the Thanksgiving holiday. Even so, I'm not questioning him right now because, honestly, I don't have the energy. I'll be home soon, and I know once I'm there I'll feel more like talking about whatever's bothering him—other than my fake pregnancy scare.

"I'm sorry about this, Jack. I'll explain everything tomorrow when I get home." If it were a few hours earlier, I'd leave today, but my parents would have a fit if I tried to head home now.

"Fine, but I'll probably be at the shop when you get home. If you're still awake when I get in, we can talk." His emotions must have settled some because the tone of his voice is almost back to normal, which gives me a little relief.

"Do you want me to stop by the shop on my way home?" I

chew on my bottom lip and pace the small space of the bathroom.

"No, you'll be tired from the drive. I'll just see you when I get in." My heart plummets into my stomach. *What if I don't care if I'm tired? I just want to see you.*

"Yeah, okay. I'll text you before I leave in the morning." That's kind of our thing if I ever travel without him or he without me. We text only after we're in the car, seat belt on, car idling and ready to leave, and then we text again if we stop for bathroom breaks or food.

"Yep. Be safe," he says. A chime resonates through the phone, and I know someone just walked into the shop. "Someone just walked in. Talk to you later." The call ends, and all I can do is stare at the screen. What just happened? I know it was partially my fault, but he chose not to give me time to explain myself. He only saw the worst-case scenario, which was either me thinking I was pregnant and not telling him or there being a chance I could be pregnant.

We'll work it out. I love him. He loves me. He's my forever, even if he doesn't realize it yet.

4

JOVIE

Three weeks before Christmas

"You haven't had sex in how long?" Layla asks loudly.

I scan the large room quickly, taking in the nameless faces and hoping no one heard her. Since Layla and I both have the day off, we decided to meet up at Jake's Bar for a quick chat before she has to meet with the florist for some wedding planning stuff. "Dammit, Layla, there's no reason to tell everyone in here that my boyfriend hasn't touched me in almost two weeks," I whisper, overcompensating for my loudmouthed friend. I realize two weeks doesn't sound like a terribly long time, but for us it's like an eternity. I can't remember the last time we went longer than four days.

"Do you think it's the pregnancy scare?" she asks as she sips her Long Island Iced Tea.

"There was no pregnancy scare. I told you what happened. Did you forget in all your wedding planning bliss?" I narrow my eyes at her before tucking a loose strand of hair behind my ear.

My body tenses at the memory of Jack's reaction after I sat him down and explained the entire scenario. I thought he would get a good laugh out of it and life would return to normal, but he mostly just avoided the subject after I finished my spiel, instead asking about Mom and her recovery. I guess I need to be happy that he's kind of sweeping it under the rug, but it's concerning that he didn't even want to discuss it. I plan on eventually bringing it up again. Maybe. Crap, I don't know. It's over and done with, so I'll probably just drop it... unless of course he brings it up again.

Layla giggles and turns toward me on the barstool where she's sitting. "I didn't forget, but I was thinking that even though it really wasn't a scare to you, it was to Jack. You said y'all have never discussed having kids or what would happen if you accidentally got pregnant, right?"

I nod as I scoot in closer to her. I'm done with everyone in this room hearing all about my problems. "I've always been on the pill, and he knows that, so we've never had a reason to talk about it."

She leans in and then covers my hand, which is resting on the countertop with hers. "Jack loves you, and I promise all of this will work itself out. You're both under a lot of stress." She lifts her lips, giving me a small smile. "You've been crazy busy with finals, and he's been working more, so it's understandable for y'all to be a little off right now."

"I don't want to be off. I want everything to be the way it's been forever. It's not like I've never had finals before. I've been in school since we started dating." I slip my hand from underneath hers, grab my Diet Coke, and take a long pull from the straw. The cool liquid slides down my throat, but it doesn't give me what I need. What I need is about four shots of tequila and a gallon of ice cream, but that's a no-go because I try not to day drink, and also, my ass wouldn't appreciate the calories that would come with the false sense of comfort I'd get from the sugary rush of my favorite rocky road treat.

I set my drink down and suck in a deep breath. "And it's not like this is the first time Jack's had to work more hours. I mean, any time one of the guys or Annie takes a vacation, he almost always volunteers to work." I rest my elbow on the ledge of the bar as I move in even closer to my friend. "It's just that nothing has ever interfered with our sex life. I mean *nothing*, and it's scaring me."

"I don't think Jack would ever—"

"Don't even say it." I cut her off because we are not going down that road. Jack is not a cheater, and I will not allow her to even say the words out loud. My motto is to never verbalize something terrible because then it puts it out there in the world to possibly happen.

"How do you know what I was going to say?" Her perfectly shaped eyebrows scrunch together. "I could've been going to say I don't think Jack would ever go an entire month without having sex. For Christ's sake, Jovie, it's only been two weeks. Don't always assume the worst." She wiggles on her stool before taking another sip of her drink.

"I call bullshit. You know that's not what you were going to say." I know and she knows she was going to hint that maybe Jack's doing something he shouldn't, like seeing someone else or hooking up with random girls. *Dammit!* This is what I don't want. I don't want to think about the idea of him doing anything that would involve cheating because he wouldn't, and I know it. That said, I'm worried Layla may not be as confident about it as I am. Hell, she's marrying a guy who's in a rock band and never worries. Why can't I be the type of person who never worries? *Because your anxiety won't allow it.*

"How do you know? Geez, sometimes I think you enjoy worrying about shit that's out of your control."

"Out of my control, huh? We'll have to see about that." I grin smugly.

Layla hops off her barstool and stands directly in front of me before raising an eyebrow. "I know that look, Jovie Blake. You're up to something."

"I'm not up to anything." She knows me too well. She's right, I am up to something, but dammit, I don't have a choice. Either I worry myself into a panic attack or I nip this little problem in the bud.

"I'm your best friend, so there's no need to bullshit me. Spill."

I grab her wrists and pull her in a bit closer, and the smile on her face grows.

"I scheduled an appointment for a tattoo," I say with a little apprehension, because let's face it—how hard up do you have to be to schedule an appointment to see your boyfriend?

"Another tattoo? When did you decide to do that? And why haven't you mentioned it?"

I release her wrists and she steps away from me. "Hello! I'm not really getting a tattoo. I scheduled the appointment so I could spend an hour or so with Jack."

"Oh... I think that's a great idea." She waggles her eyebrows and smiles.

"Really? Because I was a little worried about the whole idea of tricking him into spending time with me." I hate that my voice sounds so insecure, but a part of me feels like an idiot to have done this—although another part of me feels like it's the best idea ever.

"Absolutely. You'll have an hour alone with him inside his station with the door shut and locked. I'd make the most of that time—if you know what I mean." Her smile transforms into a smirk.

My original plan was to take my scheduled appointment time and spend it hanging out and talking, just basically having some us time, something we both need desperately. I wasn't planning to lock him in a room and screw his brains out for an hour, but now that she suggests it....

"Are you proposing that I lock my boyfriend in his station and then seduce him?" My teeth pull at my bottom lip as my mind runs a million miles a minute considering all the possibilities.

Layla leans against the bar and crosses her ankles. "Who said anything about seduce? You're past that point in the relationship. You need to walk into his station, close and lock the door, and then take back what's yours." Her eyes widen and grow bright. "Wow, that sounded really hot, huh?"

I nod. "Yep, and I'm not going to sit around and watch our relationship deteriorate. It's time for me to make something happen instead of waiting on him."

"That's my girl." She chuckles. "You go take your man back, and then we've got a wedding to plan." She winks and gives me a quick hug. Layla grabs her phone from the bar, looks down at the screen, and tenses. "Speaking of weddings, I've got to run. I have a meeting with the florist in ten minutes."

"Go, go!" I say as she rushes toward the exit.

"We'll talk about this later, and I want all the details!" she shouts as she disappears out the door.

5

JOVIE

Two weeks before Christmas

I pull open the door to Southern Stain with a shaky hand. I've yet to understand why I'm so nervous. I've been here to visit Jack a hundred times over the last few years. I've even hung out with him for hours while he worked alone, helping him answer the phone and wait on customers while he was busy creating his art in the back. For some reason, though, today feels different, like I'm doing something wrong.

I step inside the building, take a deep breath, and then slowly release it. Then I run my sweating palms over the short pleated skirt I'm wearing. I glance down at my red Mary Janes and black socks that are a little longer than knee-highs but don't quite reach my thighs. This is not my typical daily attire, but it's one of Jack's favorites—even though I can't remember the last time I wore it during the day.

"Jovie, hey." Annie's voice floats across the room as she

makes her way to me. Annie is Jack's best friend. They grew up together in Dallas and moved to Houston after high school. When Jack and I first started dating, it seemed weird for him to have a female best friend, but it didn't take me long to realize their relationship was just like mine and Layla's. Their friendship has never caused any problems for us, and actually, Annie and I have become really close too.

"Hi. Is Jack busy?" I ask, knowing if he is then he should be finishing up because my appointment is at two o'clock and it's currently five minutes till.

"Hmm...." She looks over her shoulder down the long hallway toward his station. "I'm not sure. Did he know you were coming?" She walks across the lobby, eating up the distance between us.

I'm kind of at a loss for words because I'm embarrassed to tell her I made an appointment, but I don't want to lie and let her assume he knew I was coming because he didn't or doesn't. Shit, now my stomach is in knots and my knees are wobbly. I just need to see Jack, and then I'll feel better; plus I'm sure he has no clue I'm even on his schedule unless he checked it, which I know he never checks his daily itinerary.

"No, he's not expecting me, but...." Deep laughter cuts me off before my gaze moves from Annie to the long hallway leading to my boyfriend's station.

Jack. I'd recognize his voice anywhere. A light airy tone follows his as Jack and a tall blonde step out of his station. The blonde touches his arm before saying something that's obviously funny because their laughter continues as they move toward the lobby. I understand what my boyfriend does for a living. He creates art on the bodies of both men and women. Sometimes it's in a place where everyone can see, and sometimes it's not. He's seen tits in every size, butt cheeks, and even skin that is usually covered by panties. I pride myself on not being a jealous girlfriend. This is his job. I trust him completely, but today it feels like something different.

The blonde is wearing tight skinny jeans with heels, and her legs go on forever. I swear they're twice as long as mine. Her tank is red and fits snuggly across her chest—her very large chest. As she gets closer, I notice the writing on it says Southern Stain. *Wait a second...* I glance over at Annie, and she forces a smile onto her face. My eyes move to her T-shirt, which has the same Southern Stain logo as the one gracing the tank. I'm kind of confused as to who this woman is. She's definitely a woman, most likely late twenties or early thirties—closer to Jack's age than mine.

Jack continues to make his way to the lobby while chatting with the blonde. He still hasn't seen me, and it's probably because the counter is blocking his vision. I'm certain it's not because he's so engrossed in conversation that he doesn't realize there are other people in the shop.

Annie's eyes flit from me to Jack and then back to me. "He's been training the new girl," she whispers, so softly I'm certain no one else heard her.

The new girl? What new girl? Jack has never said anything about a new girl. My mind's racing, and my breaths are short and choppy. *Oh shit.* I squeeze my eyes closed and focus on my breathing in an attempt to stop the anxiety attack before it hits. Sometimes this works and sometimes it doesn't, but I'm going to try my hardest not to let this conversation throw me into a full-blown meltdown. I refuse to have a panic attack over something

I've manifested in my mind. *Jack hasn't touched me in weeks. The fake pregnancy scare. He's never home. Stop doing this to yourself. Your mind is your worst enemy.*

"Are you okay?" Annie's voice is still soft, but she's closer. Luckily, she pulls me away from my thoughts for a few seconds.

I slowly open my eyes and focus on her worried face. "Yes." *No.* I want to run away or maybe curl up in a corner somewhere, hiding from everyone and everything because of the embarrassment that follows losing control of my sanity.

"Jovie?" Jack's questioning voice draws near, and my eyes immediately travel to him. I open my mouth to speak but nothing comes out. I swallow hard around the lump in my throat as I try to fight the tingling moving up my arms and neck, settling on my left cheek. "Are you okay?" I nod because right now that's all I can manage to do.

"I'll be back in a couple of hours." The voice is the same airy tone from before, and I know it belongs to the blonde. Jack nods in her direction without speaking.

My gaze shifts from Jack to the woman as she walks out the door.

A wave of nausea hits my belly as the clammy feeling I know all too well settles over me.

"You're pale. When's the last time you had something to eat?" Annie's soft voice resonates from beside me.

"I'm fine, really. I just need to sit down for a minute," I lie. What I need to do is get back in my car and drive home, crawl up in bed, and forget I made a fool out of myself.

"Jovie," Jack whispers as he reaches for my arm. "Jovie," he repeats, pulling me into his chest. He knows what's happening, and I love him so much for trying to help me. He hates it as much as I do that this anxiety demon has so much control of my life.

I wrap my arms around his waist and rest my cheek against his chest just as the tingling starts in my fingers and moves up my arms until a twitch takes over my right eye. "It's happening, Jack, and I can't stop it," I mumble against his T-shirt.

Even though Jack saw me have an attack when I first moved to town almost four years ago, it still doesn't make me feel any better about him watching me fall apart. I squeeze my eyes closed and take deep breaths, slowly counting to ten. Jack kisses the top of my head and rubs the back of my neck gently. "It's okay, babe, just breathe. Just breathe," he says.

I'm okay. It's just anxiety. I take in a deep breath. "One. Two. Three," I mumble against Jack's hard chest. I release the breath and do it again. "One. Two. Three." And release. I feel better already. I don't know if it's my breathing exercises or because Jack's holding me; it's probably a combination of both. I slowly open my eyes, tilt my head back, and look at him. Worry is etched all over his face, and I feel like an idiot.

My plan was to wear his favorite outfit, flirt a bit, and have him fuck me against the wall in his station. But in the end, I walked in here looking like a child next to the woman he's "training," and then to top it all off, I had a freaking panic attack.

"Sorry, I don't know what happened. One minute I was fine and the next I couldn't breathe." I release my hold from around his waist, but my eyes never leave his.

"Damn, baby," he mumbles quietly as he covers his face with his hands. "You scared the shit out of me."

"Sorry, I wanted to surprise you and—" I hesitate for a beat. "Instead I ruined everything." I shake my head and look away for a couple of seconds. Why can't life go back to the way it was two months ago? What changed? Whatever it is, it's made me someone I don't want to be—insecure, needy, lonesome.

"You haven't ruined anything. I am surprised." He smirks and reaches for my hand. "Come on. Let's go talk until my next appointment shows up." He winks and tugs me down the hallway toward his station.

6

JOVIE

"I am your next appointment," I tell Jack with an unsteady voice as the door to his station closes behind us.

"What do you mean you're my next appointment?" He lets out a soft chuckle, like he thinks I'm joking, before reaching around me and securing the lock.

My insides tremble as I wrestle with how I'm going to explain how I wanted to surprise him so I just basically took money out of his pocket because I blocked off his book for the next hour.

"I went online and scheduled an appointment with you today." My gaze meets his.

He shakes his head and squints slightly. "I don't understand why you would do that unless you really want another tattoo, and even then, you should have told me so we could have done this on one of my days off." He looks puzzled, almost confused. It's obvious he's not as okay with this idea as I thought he would be when I planned it. "Do you want one… a tattoo?" He grips my wrist and moves me across the small room toward the dark leather couch in the back.

I stop walking. "No, but I also didn't mean for everything to play out the way it has since I walked through the door today."

Jack hesitates and turns to face me. "What happened out there?" He motions toward the closed door. "Did something trigger the attack?" He takes a step toward me.

"Nothing triggered it. I just suddenly started feeling overwhelmed and then... well, you know the way it works." Lies. Lies. Lies. There is no way in hell I'm telling him that seeing him being so friendly with the "new girl" sent me spiraling into a panic attack. I bite my lower lip and shift my eyes downward, looking at the floor. "I hate that I can't control my anxiety, Jack. Do you know how embarrassing it is?"

"Come here, baby." He pulls me into him and wraps his arms around me tightly. I want to scream. I want to cry. I want to be normal and live without fear of freaking out and falling apart at any given minute.

"I'm sorry about today. I've just...." I hesitate a beat and pull away from him so I can look at his face.

"You've what?" he asks, cupping my face.

"I've missed you." There, I said it, and it's the truth. I've missed him terribly. I've missed the way we were until a few short weeks ago. I want it back, and I'm willing to fight for it.

"I'm right here. I haven't been anywhere, and I'm not going anywhere." He leans in and presses his warm mouth against my cheek, brushing it lightly. A shiver races through me, hitting every single nerve ending in my entire body. It seems like it's been so long without his touch that any attention he gives me sets me on fire. "What do you want, Jovie? Just tell me and I promise I'll make it happen," he whispers against my lips.

A soft moan escapes my chest as he kisses me harder. His hands slide down my arms, leaving a trail of goose bumps. I bite and suck on his lower lip as my gaze meets his. Burning desire is all I see in his dark eyes. "Touch me," I whisper.

"Here?" He tugs at the hem of my shirt as his fingers graze my stomach. "Or here?" He lifts my skirt and toys with the elastic band of my panties. A shudder races up my spine, and the greedy side of me wants to scream "Both. Take it all!" But I don't. Instead I gather all my restraint and force myself not to rip off his clothes and just take what I want from him. I slow my breathing as I wait, playing the game with him, hoping it won't be too much longer before he can't take the torture and gives me what I came here for.

Jack's hand slips inside my panties, and I let out a groan. "Maybe you want me to touch you here." His voice is a mumble as he slides two fingers inside of me. "So fucking wet." His words vibrate against my lips.

I say his name once and then again when he presses his palm against my clit, hitting it with just enough pressure to send a volt of electricity shooting through me. I really want to show some self-control and fight off my impending orgasm, but I can't. It hits me fast and hard. "I'm coming!" My head falls back, and Jack's teeth skim my neck, biting and sucking. Hard and soft. Pain and pleasure. My body falls against his, and he lifts me from the floor, walking us toward the couch.

No words are spoken as he places me gently on the sofa. As soon as my butt hits the leather cushion, Jack drops to his knees in front of me. His hands move swiftly, taking off my blouse and tugging at my bra until it's off my body and lying on the floor.

His mouth hastily moves down my chest and settles on my left breast. My nipple pebbles underneath his touch, and that familiar ache is back between my legs. "You taste so fucking good, Jovie." His mouth continues to move across my chest, giving my right breast the same attention he gave my left. He slowly kisses his way up my chest and neck until his lips reach mine.

"Take off your clothes and fuck me," I whisper before pushing him away.

Jack hops to his feet, his eyes never leaving mine. His lips pull into a half smile as he rips the T-shirt from his body and tosses it to the side. His jeans and boxer briefs follow, and then he's standing here, with his long beautiful cock pointing directly at me. A few minutes ago, all I could think about was feeling him inside of me, but now I need to lick him, taste him, make him feel as good as he made me feel a few minutes ago.

I scoot to the edge of the couch, moving my gaze to his. Jack takes two steps toward me, and I grip his erection.

Bang, bang, bang! "Hey, Jack! I need you out here." Annie's voice echoes from the other side of the door.

You've got to be kidding me. My eyes flit from Jack's erection to his face. He looks irritated, almost pained.

"Fuck!" Jack hollers out in frustration. His body tenses, but his gaze never leaves mine. "Can't it wait a few minutes?" he asks Annie in an irritated yell.

I lean forward and lick the glistening head of his cock. He lets out a grunt before dragging his fingers through my hair. I watch him watching me as I lick the underside of his shaft from root to crown. "Fuck, baby," he moans.

"No, it can't wait." Annie's still talking, but it's not slowing us down. I suck harder, and the need between my legs grows. I lift my skirt and slide my hand inside my panties, stopping only when my fingers sweep over my clit. My body jerks slightly at the sensation.

"Pull them down. I want to watch." Jack's voice is thick and heavy.

My mouth continues to torture him in the best possible way as I wiggle out of my panties, giving him what he wants.

Bang, bang, bang! "It's Mr. Thomas. He's here to see you, and he can't come back!" Annie yells, her voice laced with frustration. Dammit, I knew this was a bad idea. The next time I think I've got a good idea, I need to reevaluate it closely before I act upon it.

Jack immediately pulls away from me and grabs his clothes. "Sorry, babe. I've got to go." He bends over and kisses me on the lips before dressing. "I'll make it up to you tonight."

My skin is still on fire, and my heart hasn't slowed from its race inside my chest because my body thinks there is going to be more, but unfortunately there's not. God, I want to be pissed, but how can I justify being upset with Jack. This is his job, and the man waiting on him is more than likely a customer.

"Who is Mr. Thomas?" I ask, trying to hide my disappointment.

Jack looks at me and hesitates a beat before answering. "A client."

Wow. He actually had to think about that answer.

"He didn't have an appointment, right? I mean, I had the whole hour, and it's only been thirty minutes."

"Do you think I wanted this to end?" Jack motions between the two of us before moving toward the door.

"Well, I mean… no." *I hope not.*

He stops and turns back to look at me. "Exactly, but I don't have a choice. I'm at work. We shouldn't have—" He runs a hand through his hair. "I shouldn't have let it go as far as it did. I'm sorry, but I've got a customer waiting." He walks out the door, leaving me half naked and alone.

I don't know how I'm supposed to feel. My body's numb and my mind is sifting through what just happened. I get dressed and head toward the lobby. Annie is leaning against the counter, staring at her phone. "See ya later," I tell her as I pass by.

"Oh, bye, Jovie." She pushes off the counter and walks toward me. "It was good to see you."

I open my mouth to speak, but movement to my right grabs my attention. I glance over in that direction to see Jack talking with an older gentleman. The man is balding, and he's wearing a blue and white striped button-down shirt, a dark gray tie, and dress slacks. He's holding a folder in one hand and an ink pen in the other. Hmm... Mr. Thomas? He doesn't look like one of Jack's typical clients. Actually, I bet Mr. Thomas has never stepped foot in a tattoo studio until today. Jack catches me watching and throws me a small smile then immediately returns his attention to the man standing in front of him.

I look back over my shoulder at Annie, who has stopped walking in my direction and is back to staring at her phone screen. I huff out a breath then push through the door and head toward my car.

7

JOVIE

One week before Christmas

"Thanks for coming to the party with me," I whisper to Jack as I touch my lips softly to his.

He pulls back slightly and grins. "Anything for you. Now, let's get inside before we get wet." A distant rumbling in the darkness, followed by lightning dancing across the night sky, reminds me that a storm is heading this way. I stuff my hands inside the pockets of my coat and shiver.

Jack tugs open the door to Jake's Bar and motions for me to enter. Cheap Christmas lights are strung around the place, there are several blow-up decorations meant for someone's front yard and not the inside of a bar, and the band, Nocturnal Revolution, is making their way on stage to get the Christmas music started. Jake throws a festive party for most holidays—New Year's, Valentine's Day, Fourth of July, Labor Day, Memorial Day, Thanksgiving, and Christmas—with Christmas being my favorite.

I take my coat off and hang it on one of the many hooks near the door then rub my cold hands on my jean-covered legs. The temperature is not much warmer inside than outside.

Jack wraps his arms around me, pulling me into his warm body. "You cold?" He kisses the top of my head. I want to tell him yes, say I'm freezing so maybe he'll hold me like this for the rest of the night, but we're here to spend time with our friends, and I know he needs to enjoy his rare night off.

"A little, but not too bad." I force myself to step away from him so he can mingle with the crowd. Hanging out with his friends is something he doesn't do often. Actually, it's something both of us only do occasionally. Between school, work, and studying for me and his recent long hours, neither of us have much spare time.

Nocturnal Revolution starts the night off with "All I Want for Christmas Is You," and I feel like they're playing it for me as my gaze meets Jack's.

"I'm gonna make the rounds and have a drink. If you want, we can head out after that, maybe spend the rest of the night just you and me at home." He winks and my heart melts.

I nod and smile. "Sure, sounds good." I'm so giddy right now I can hardly contain myself. Everything is changing... in a good way. I finally feel like I'm getting my boyfriend back. The last week has been so much better—at least the sex part has. He's still been working into the early hours of the morning, but the difference is that I'm not in school, so I nap during the afternoon, and then I'm able to stay up and wait for him. My mind hasn't completely let go of the worry, but I've conditioned myself to not be completely consumed by all the what-ifs.

He walks toward the bar, and I scan the room in search of

Layla. I blow out a deep breath, tuck a strand of hair behind my ear, and take a couple of steps toward the crowd.

"Jovie, is that you?" A deep, familiar voice sounds from behind me. Crap, it's Stone. He's my least favorite of Jack's friends, but he is Jack's friend and boss, so I put on my best fake grin and turn to face him.

My smile fades as I take in the woman on his right. The blonde from Southern Stain— "the new girl"—is staring at me, 100 percent focused on my face. I meet her eyes, refusing to let her arrogance make me feel intimidated, because I'm not. Her lip twitches a couple of times before a smug grin finds her face.

"It is you," Stone says loudly.

"Yep, it's me," I tell him as I pull my gaze from the blonde to look at him.

He glances at the woman to his right and then back at me. "Jovie, have you met my cousin Candi?" Cousin? Great, that means she's going to be around for a while. *Of course she is—Jack was "training her," so it's safe to assume she works for Stone.*

"No," I answer, because I don't want to explain how I saw her at the shop in the middle of a panic attack and she ran out the door before I was able to regain my sanity.

"We have met," Candi says before hesitating for a beat. "Well, we weren't actually introduced, but I think you came into the shop last week. Right?"

"Oh, yeah, you're right, but you were leaving just as I got there." I cross my arms over my chest. The chill I had when we walked in the building is suddenly gone and replaced with what feels like an inferno burning inside of me.

"Yeah, that's right. You're Jack's girlfriend?" It comes out more like a question than a statement.

I force a smile and then nod before Stone proceeds to tell me what I've already figured out.

"Candi's gonna be working part-time with us at the shop," he says, pulling my attention from Candi. Nice, just what I wanted to hear—part-time Candi, who my boyfriend is training.

"Hey, sweetheart, sorry I'm late. Got held up at the hospital." A tall, slender man walks up next to Candi, wrapping his arm around her waist before leaning in and kissing her lips.

My gaze travels to the older, attractive, dark-haired man to Candi's left. Shit, I never even noticed the ring on her finger. I'm so stupid. I let my insecurity get the best of me. *Not everybody is after your man, dumbass.*

"Tad, I'm so glad you made it." Stone reaches in front of Candi to shake the man's hand.

"Me too—the ER was crazy tonight." The man's gaze meets mine and he smiles. "And you are?"

"This is Jack's girlfriend, Jovie," Stone replies, not giving me a chance to answer.

"Hi, nice to meet you," I say, hoping someone will suddenly appear and save me from the awkwardness I'm feeling.

"Tad is an emergency medicine doctor over at Mercy General," Stone adds.

"Are you going to stand in the entryway all night? Or do you plan on making it over to say hi to Layla?" Jack wraps his arms around my waist and rests his chin on my shoulder.

I grab hold of his hands and squeeze. *Thank you for saving me.* "No, I was hanging out near the door waiting for you to finish whatever it is you're doing so we can go home," I whisper, remembering his promise of going home early.

His deep chuckle against my neck sends a shudder down my spine. He kisses my cheek before directing his attention to the three standing in front of us. "Tad, Candi, Stone," Jack acknowledges the trio.

Candi's smugness remains throughout the few minutes of small talk between the group, and I decide maybe she's just arrogant, possibly because she's married to a doctor. Maybe she grew up wealthy. I don't know, and honestly, I don't really care if she's the sweetest woman in the world or the meanest bitch in this bar. It doesn't matter because any thought I had about her having a thing for my boyfriend is gone. I'm done letting my insecurities manifest shit that's not true.

The trio disperses into the crowd, and I spin around in Jack's arms to face him. "Were you serious about leaving early?" I ask.

"Yep, I'd rather be home in bed with you than hanging out with the same people I see all the time." He pulls me in closer and whispers near my ear, "I've missed you, Jovie."

"I've missed you too," I whisper.

"Let's go home." He slides a hand down my arm and clasps his fingers with mine, leading me toward the door, only stopping so I can grab my coat. Jack pushes the door open and we head for his Jeep.

8

JOVIE

I slam the door to Jack's Jeep about two seconds before the rain begins to fall. The lightning decorates the dark sky in front of us as thunder rolls just outside my door.

"We barely made it," Jack says as he cranks up the engine and turns on the heater. "Are you cold?" He touches my face softly before skimming my jaw and neck with his finger. My entire body trembles from the softness of his touch. "Come here, baby." He gently tugs on my neck, pulling me closer to him. His mouth slants over mine. God, I swear he tastes like happiness and pleasure.

The rain continues to beat down on the windshield, and the wind gusts begin to rock the vehicle. Jack pulls back and stares into my eyes. "Home," I tell him before he starts up another make-out session. As much as I love kissing him, I'd really like more—a whole lot more, and a whole lot more is not something I want to do in the parking lot at Jake's.

"Yes, ma'am." He chuckles as he fastens his seat belt. Jack leans over and checks mine to be sure I'm secured in. It's something he always does, I guess out of habit. He slowly pulls out of the parking lot just before a loud clap of thunder roars.

"Dammit!" My heart bangs around in my chest and my pulse soars.

"You okay?" Jack asks, never taking his eyes off the road.

"Yeah, I guess I wasn't expecting it to sound like it was in the vehicle with us." I blow out a long, slow breath, rest my head against the cool leather of the seat, and close my eyes.

"There's something I wanted to talk to you about. I've been putting it off, and I—" Jack's voice cracks, but he's already said enough to get my attention. I open my eyes and jerk up, turning slightly in my seat so I can see him. Whatever he's going to say, I want to be able to see him so I can watch his emotions as they move over his face.

Lightning blazes across the sky, and I get a glimmer of his profile. His eyes squint as a truck flies past us, throwing more water on the windshield. I touch his arm lightly and give it a squeeze. "Hey, whatever it is you want to say, it can wait until we get home." I don't know why he decided talking about something that's obviously important right now while driving through a storm is a good idea. "I know driving in the rain makes you nervous."

We're about twenty minutes from home, and that's on a clear, sunny day without any traffic, so I'm sure we're about to spend an hour or more in this storm, especially with Jack driving. He's always careful and extremely cautious with me in the car, but with it storming, he'll definitely take it up a notch.

"I thought maybe if we talked it would take my mind off the storm," he says.

"We can talk. I just would rather save anything that's important or might cause you any additional stress until we get home." I move my hand to his jean-covered leg and rub it gently. "Hey, why don't you let me drive?"

I'm not particularly fond of driving in the rain but watching him hold his breath as he white-knuckles the steering wheel driving twenty miles per hour is not something I can endure for the entire trip home.

He laughs, but it's forced. "I'm fine, Jovie. I'll have you home safe and sound before you know it." His voice never wavers, but actions speak a whole lot louder than the words he just spoke, and judging by his recent gestures, I'd say he's nervous.

I huff out a breath and rest my head against the passenger window.

The driver's side front tire hits a puddle of water and pulls the Jeep to the right just as the driver behind us lays on their horn. "Fuck!" Jack hollers.

It's really weird how anxiety works. You would think I'd be terrified, curled up in a ball in my seat crying, but I'm fine. Storms normally aren't a trigger for me, but stick me in a supermarket with a hundred other people and I have to leave my buggy full of groceries in the middle of the store and go home before having a breakdown.

"Please, Jack, pull over and let me drive. I don't like to see you so stressed," I plead. This is so not my boyfriend, but I know why he's this way. The night Piper died, there wasn't any rain, thunder, or lightning, only a drunk driver, and that man took so much from so many people. I honestly didn't think Jack would ever let me ride in a vehicle he was driving.

He doesn't say anything as he pulls over to the shoulder of

the road. The Jeep rolls to a stop, and Jack shakes his head a couple of times before resting it on the steering wheel, defeated.

My heart aches for him. "Jack," I whisper, because honestly, I don't really know what to say. I can't stand to see him like this.

He throws the vehicle in park, opens his door, and steps out into the pouring rain. Why does life have to be so damn hard?

I quickly move over into the seat Jack just vacated and adjust the seat and mirror. He slams the passenger door, and my eyes jerk to him. "Are you okay?" I ask, my eyes glassy from the tears I'm fighting.

Water drips from his hair, rolls down his face, and drops onto his soaked, long-sleeved, gray Henley. Pursed lips and a tense jawline are all I can make out. I want him to look at me so I know he's okay, but he doesn't. He only spits out two words as he latches his seat belt. "Just drive."

My body trembles and my vision wavers as I try to fight back the tears. I put the Jeep in drive, look over my shoulder to be sure the road is clear, and then pull out onto the highway. I just want to get home, crawl in bed, and wrap up in Jack. He'll smile and tell me he loves me, and we'll forget all about this stupid drive.

Lights flicker in front of me, but they don't look like taillights. I squint, lean forward a bit, and then use one hand to wipe the fog from the window. The lights seem to be getting closer. I glance over at Jack, who is resting his head against the seat with his eyes closed. *Shit!* When I bring my gaze back to the road, it's too late. The lights are directly in front of me and they're connected to a car going the wrong direction down the highway. "Jack!" I scream as I jerk the steering wheel to the right and then slam on the brakes, trying to avoid them, but it's too late. A clap of thunder screams loudly somewhere in the darkness. Crunching metal pulls at my ears as burning rubber twists and curls, stinging my nose. My head is heavy and my vision blurs once, twice, and on the third time, everything goes dark.

9

JOVIE

Then

Christmas Eve

"Santa Claus won't come if you don't go to sleep," Piper whispers, and I laugh loudly. "Shh!" She presses her finger against her lips as she makes the noise. "You're gonna wake up Mom and Dad."

She climbs into my bed and lies down beside me, resting her head on my oversized pillow.

"No, I won't. Daddy went to the station to check on something important, and Mom is passed out. I think she drank too much of her relaxation drink again." I laugh again, but this time I'm not as loud. "Oh, and Santa will come even if I'm awake," I tell her as she snuggles against me.

"Who told you that?" she asks.

"Nobody, but I'm not stupid, you know. I'm twelve, not two. And I also know—"

"Don't say it!" She looks at me pointedly. "If you don't believe then—"

"I know, I know—then I won't get any presents."

"That's right, little sister. And speaking of presents, what are your thoughts on our gifts this year? Did you ask for anything good?"

I wiggle around in the bed until I'm propped up against the headrest looking at Piper. This is our thing. We always spend Christmas Eve in either my bed or hers. We talk and laugh until sleep takes us away.

"Nope. Not this year. I told Mom and Dad to surprise me."

"Surprise you?" Piper questions as she fluffs her pillow and then readjusts her head.

"Yeah, I'm tired of always knowing what I'm getting. I think it takes all the fun out of it. So, this year, I have no idea what's under the tree, and I'm more excited than ever."

"Hmm... that's pretty good thinking, sis." She laughs softly.

My mind reels from one subject to the next, stopping at my mom and her drinking problem. I may only be twelve, but I know walking around every morning with a bottle of vodka in one hand and a cup of coffee in the other is not normal behavior. What bothers me the most is that no one ever talks about it. We just carry on with our life like everything is okay. Since my big sister is in a great mood, I decide to give it a shot and ask the question that is always on my mind. "Do you think Mom will ever stop drinking?"

"Wow. Subject change, huh?" Her eyes lose a little of their brightness at the mention of Mom's problem with alcohol. We all know it's real, but no one—including our dad—will talk to us about it. He says eventually she'll get better. I may be a kid, but

I'm not stupid. She struggles every day, and it makes me really sad for her.

"I don't know. Maybe one day. It'll probably take something bad happening before she stops for good." She shrugs with one shoulder. "That's the way it usually works."

"Hopefully you're right. I mean about the part where she stops drinking, not about the something bad happening." Somewhere buried deep inside my brain, I know something bad will happen and it will give Mom a reason to stop drinking for a long time, but she'll eventually go back to the bottle time and time again.

My mind drifts in and out of sleep. Piper kisses me on the forehead. "Good night, Jovie. I love you." Her voice is soft, and it sounds like she's far away.

"I love you too, Piper, and I miss you every day. We all do." Tears pool behind my eyes as they flutter open briefly, a few tears escaping before they close on their own.

"I miss you too, little sis, but everything's good. I promise." Her voice drifts even farther away.

I whisper her name. She doesn't answer, so I say her name again and again. Each time it's a little louder. Still no answer. I reach my hand out to touch her, but she's not there. The empty space beside me is cold. *I miss you too,* hovers in the air around me.

"Live your best life and love with your whole heart." Her voice fades away with the last few words, and I know she's gone forever. *Open your eyes, Jovie.*

10

JOVIE

Now

Christmas Eve

My eyes jerk open, and I suck in a deep breath. *Piper.* I squeeze my eyes closed for a couple of seconds before opening them again. *Beep, beep, beep.* What's that noise? I move my head slowly to the right and take in the large window. There's no light filtering through the blinds, so it must be dark outside. *Beep, beep, beep.* Where's that sound coming from? "Where am I?" I mumble, my voice sounding hoarse and weak.

"Jovie?" The familiar female voice grabs my attention. *Mom.*

"Mom, where am I?" I blink my eyes a few times, and she's standing over me. Her eyes are red, swollen, and tears are streaming down her face.

Suddenly I'm blindsided by so many emotions, but the main one is fear. The storm, the car going the wrong direction, the burning rubber... Jack. My heart slams around in my chest as my pulse races through my veins. The air is heavy, and I can't breathe. "Where's Jack? Mom, please... where is he?" In just the few seconds that my eyes have been open, my mind has manifested every worst-case scenario possible.

"I'm here, Jovie." His voice is laced with relief.

I let out a huge breath as I reach for him. "Jack," I mutter as my eyes fill with tears.

Mom steps to the side as he approaches the bed, leaning down and swallowing me in a big hug. "Thank God you're awake," he whispers near my ear before kissing my cheek, and I cry. The tears continue to fall as he pulls back from the hug and stares into my eyes. "Don't ever scare me like this again."

I scrunch my nose, sniffle, and nod. I'm still not completely myself. I feel drugged—groggy and still fighting sleep—but I'm so thankful I'm still here, that the accident wasn't as bad as it could have been.

Jack has a couple of lacerations on his face that have been stitched closed and a healing bruise underneath his left eye. I drag my hands through his hair before skimming his face with my touch. "You're okay?" I ask, my voice shaky.

"Baby, I'm fine. You're what's important, and I swear I'll spend the rest of my life taking care of you."

"Jovie, you're awake?" My dad's question cuts Jack off as he walks into the room. Jack releases me, and I want to grab him and beg him not to let me go. *I swear I'll spend the rest of my life taking care of you.*

"Yes, and I think I'm okay." At least I think I'm fine, but actually I have no idea—I'm not even sure what today is or how long I've been drifting in and out of sleep.

"Thank God." His hand trembles as he grabs me, pulling me

into a hug. "You scared the shit out of us, sweetheart." He releases me and shakes his head. "I never want to get another phone call in the middle of the night. You understand?" His light laughter is forced, fake, and I know without him saying it that receiving a phone call about me being in an accident brought back memories of the night Piper was killed.

"I never want you to get another middle-of-the-night phone call about me," I tell him. My mouth is dry, and my throat feels thick. "Mom?" I know she's still here, but she's been pushed aside by the men in my life.

"I'm right here, Jovie." She grips my hand and pushes past Dad to get to my side. "Do you feel okay? What do you need?" She may not have won any mother of the year awards when I was younger, but she's still a mom—my mom—and she just knows I need her.

"I have a bit of a headache, and my face kind of hurts." I rub my jaw then open and close it a couple of times. Honestly, I didn't realize I had any pain until just now. When I first woke up, I was so worried about Jack and then happy he was okay that I couldn't focus on anything else.

"Let me call your nurse," Dad says, reminding everyone in the room that I probably need to be checked out now that I'm awake and alert.

"Do you think I can have something to drink? My mouth feels like it's full of cotton." I direct my question toward Mom.

"I'm sure it'll be okay, but let's ask the nurse first," she answers without hesitation.

A petite brunette dressed in scrubs enters the room and makes her way to my bedside. "Hi, Jovie. I'm Tabitha, and I'll be taking care of you tonight. Does anything hurt?" Her voice is calm, almost soothing. She doesn't give me time to answer before she sticks a thermometer in my mouth, presses a few buttons on the monitor above the bed, and grabs my wrist.

I wait until she removes the thermometer before giving her the same answer I gave Mom a little while ago. Headache and face ache—if that's even a real complaint. She pours me a small cup of water and gives me some acetaminophen for the pain before explaining to everyone that she will get in touch with the doctor and let him know I'm awake and alert. She asks me a few more questions about my pain before she leaves the four of us alone again.

I love my parents and I'm grateful they drove in from Georgia, but I want everyone to leave. I'm still exhausted and fighting sleep.

"Do you think we need to hang around for the doctor so he can give us an update?" Dad directs the question toward my mother, who is sitting next to me, holding my hand. I glance over at Jack; he's leaning against the wall, quietly watching everything unfold from a distance.

"What time is it?" I briefly remember that I have no idea the time or even the day.

"It's—" Dad hesitates as he looks at the wall in front of me. "—six o'clock in the evening." He motions toward the clock hanging there—the one I didn't see.

"I bet with it being this late in the day on Christmas Eve, the doctor probably won't be back around," Mom adds.

"Wait, what? It's Christmas Eve?" My gaze flits from Mom to Jack. He smiles and then gives me a nod. "I've been out for an entire week?" I continue to look at my boyfriend.

He opens his mouth to speak, but my mom cuts him off. "You haven't really been out as in unconscious. They gave you medicine to help you rest until the doctors knew for certain that you were okay." She squeezes my hand gently. "You've actually been kind of in and out the entire time."

"I don't understand."

"What she means is that you would wake up and mumble a few words and then drift back to sleep. I think the longest you were awake at one time was maybe five minutes or so, but you weren't alert like you are now," Dad explains.

"I guess we'll head back to the hotel for the night, since you're awake. We just didn't want to both be gone until we knew you were okay," Mom says with tears still in her eyes.

"You'll be back tomorrow?" Even though I desperately need some alone time with Jack, I want to see my parents on Christmas Day.

"Of course we will," Mom answers, glancing toward my father. "Unless you want us to stay tonight."

Jack's voice interrupts. "I'm staying."

It's weird how those two words completely fill my heart with love and security. Jack's staying—with me. I'm not sure happiness is the emotion I should feel right now, but life is too short to dwell on what could have happened. I'll take the few bruises, abrasions, aches, and pains over a lifetime of loss any day.

"Thank you." My eyes flit to his, and he nods.

My parents gather their things before saying their goodbyes to me and Jack. As soon as they're gone, my boyfriend is at my bedside with my hand in his. Suddenly I'm tired, so tired I can barely keep my eyes open.

"Will you be upset with me if I go to sleep?" My eyelids are growing heavier by the second.

"I'll be upset with you if you fight sleep because of me," Jack says before kissing my forehead. "Go to sleep, Jovie. I'll be here all night if you need me."

I blink a few more times before giving up the battle and drifting off to sleep.

11

JOVIE

Christmas Day

"Merry Christmas, baby," Jack whispers, his warm breath dancing across the skin below my ear.

I rub my eyes, turn my head to face him, and smile. "Merry Christmas."

His fingers skim across my bare arm then slide in between mine, squeezing my hand gently.

"Did you sleep good?"

I nod. "Yeah, actually I did." I don't remember much after drifting off to sleep last night, which I usually equate to a good night's sleep.

"How about you? Was the couch good to you?" I motion toward the small sofa beside the bed and cringe. There is no way anyone could sleep well on that tiny thing, but knowing Jack, he'll lie and say he did just so I won't feel bad that he stayed the night.

He barks out a laugh before rubbing his neck. "I slept better than I have in years."

"I doubt that." I hesitate for a second. "But thank you... for staying."

"You couldn't have made me leave even if you wanted to."

I never want you to leave. Promise me you'll stay forever.

"How do you feel?" He brushes a strand of hair from my face.

"Good—better. I want to go home," I say softly.

"I want you to go home too, but we have to wait until the doctor says you're a 100 percent."

I'm so grateful to be alive, but for some reason I'm having to push away the poor pitiful me emotions that are pulling me in. Maybe I just need some food and a shower, and I definitely need to brush my teeth because I'm so not liking this dirty feeling I've got going on.

"Do you think I can eat something today? And maybe take a shower and brush my teeth?"

"I can't answer those questions for you, but I'll go get your nurse." He lifts my hand and kisses it gently before standing and walking out the door.

It's been a long day, especially for me since I've basically been asleep for the past few days. My parents spent most of the day here, and Layla and Sebastian came by with gifts and food. Stone, Annie, and Fish all dropped by about two hours ago but only stayed a short while. My doctor also made an appearance and gave me the not-so-great news that I can't go home today or tomorrow but maybe the next day, but he made no promises. I needed a nap and Jack knew it, so he hustled everyone out of my room so I could rest. Now I'm awake staring at my boyfriend in the chair next to the bed. His head is hanging to the side, his eyes are closed, and his breathing is slow and steady. I wonder how long he's been asleep in that position. Poor guy. He's not going to be able to hold his head up straight tomorrow. I shift my weight around in the bed to find a more comfortable position for myself, and my elbow accidentally bumps the railing. The noise is louder than I expected, and it awakens Jack. *Shit!*

"Everything okay?" he asks, jerking his head to an upright position.

"Crap, I'm sorry. I didn't mean to wake you up," I say as I turn to face him.

"It's fine. I didn't need to be sleeping here anyway. I do better on the couch." He motions toward a small sofa he slept on last night and every night since I've been here. That thought makes my heart both happy and sad—happy because he loves me enough to sacrifice his comfort, his work, and everything he needed to be doing over the past few days to stay here with me while I recover, but also sad because sleeping on that tiny pleather couch has to be miserable, especially for a guy Jack's size.

"I'm sorry about all of this." I swallow around the lump in my throat.

"Don't say that, Jovie. Don't you dare go there. None of this was your fault." He shifts around in the chair, reaches his arms above his head, and straightens his spine. "If it's anybody's fault, it's mine," he says as he lowers his arms and shifts his weight around in the chair.

"Yours?" I lean in closer to him. "How could you possibly think any of this is your fault?" I know what he's going to say before he answers because Jack blames himself for everything bad in his life, and I don't know if anything or anyone can change his thought processes.

"I never should have let you drive." He huffs out the words like he's still mad at himself.

"The accident would have happened no matter who was driving. The car that caused the accident would've still been driving on the wrong side of the road." I suck in a quick breath. "Don't blame yourself for what happened. It was an accident, and thankfully we're both okay." I scoot over to the edge of the opposite side of the bed. "Just please stop blaming yourself," I plead. "What happened to me is different. It's not the same as with Piper, and neither accident was your fault."

He nods. Jack is a good guy, the best, but he's entirely too hard on himself, and it makes me upset with him at times.

"Will you lie down with me?" I ask.

He looks over his shoulder at the door before pushing up from the chair and climbing in beside me. He wraps his strong arms around me and pulls me in close. I sigh as my body instantly relaxes into his. This is the best feeling in the entire world.

"Are you tired?" he asks, resting his chin on the top of my head.

"No, not at all. I just needed you to hold me. Is that okay?" I ask, nuzzling my face into his neck.

"Baby, it's better than okay. Honestly, I needed to hold you too," he whispers softly.

JOVIE

Three days after Christmas

I awaken early with Piper weighing heavy on my mind. She hasn't really left my thoughts since I woke up Christmas Eve night. The dream I had about her is stuck on repeat in my head. Talking about it would maybe help me to understand what it meant, but talking about it could also trigger my anxiety. I'm torn. The one thing I am sure of is that my parents are nowhere near ready to hear about all the crap going on inside my head.

"You feeling okay?" Jack asks as he walks inside my hospital room. He left for about an hour while my parents and I said our goodbyes. According to my nurse, I'm supposed to be discharged before noon today. As soon as she delivered the good news, I took a shower, brushed my teeth, and put on jeans and a sweater. Now I'm just waiting.

"Physically, I feel great." I blow out a long, slow breath.

Jack quickly walks over to where I'm sitting on the couch.

"But what? Is something wrong?" he asks, his voice laced with concern.

"No, nothing's wrong. It's just...." I bite on my bottom lip as I decide how to tell him what's going on in my mind.

"Just what, Jovie? Don't do this to me." He sits down next to me on the small sofa before adjusting his body until he's facing me. Jack rests his hand on my leg and gently squeezes. "Talk to me, baby. Please."

"Don't be upset with me, but I probably shouldn't have held it in for the last few days. It's just that there's been so much going on with my parents here and Christmas and me being so unsure of whether or not to say anything." I maneuver my body slightly so I can see him better. His dark eyes watch me as I take in a deep breath and then release it.

"Tell me what's going on." His voice is a bit stern, but I know it's only because he's worried.

"When I was sleeping or whatever it was I was doing before I woke up on Christmas Eve, I had a dream about Piper."

He drops his head downward for a beat before returning his gaze to me. "I'm listening."

"The first part of it was an exact reenactment of the last Christmas Eve we spent together before she died." Tears pool in my eyes, but I fight them because I don't want to cry yet. Jack nods but doesn't say anything. "Then I told her I loved her and missed her. She told me she missed me too but said everything was good." I squeeze my eyes closed for a second or two, and when I open them again, a single tear rolls down my cheek. "Live your best life and love with your whole heart." I'm sobbing by the time I get the last words out. "Those were her last words. Live your best life and love with your whole heart. Jack, she felt so real, like she was in the bed with me." My words taper off into silence as he pulls me into his chest and squeezes me tight.

"It's okay, baby. Just cry. I've got you, and I'm not going anywhere." His words are muffled by the sounds of my own sobs.

Jack holds me until I'm pretty much all cried out. Then he cups my face, his gaze meeting mine. His eyes are full of worry and love and sorrow. "I love you, Jovie, and I swear we will get through this together." He presses his warm lips to mine, and his kiss is a promise of forever.

EPILOGUE

JACK

New Year's Eve

I'll be the first to admit the past few months have been some of the most difficult for my relationship with Jovie, but when two people love each other as much as we do, nothing can break them apart. Houston is overflowing with New Year's Eve parties tonight, and even though Jovie hasn't been out of the hospital a full week, she's determined for us to go out. Personally, I don't think it's a good idea, but I'm gonna let her get dressed up, and then I'm taking her somewhere she'll remember forever.

"Jack, are you ready? Layla said she and Sebastian are already at Stone's house. You know I don't like to be late!" Jovie yells from the living room.

"Hold on a sec. I'm almost ready." I grab my keys from the bedside table and make my way down the short hallway into the living room.

"You look so handsome," she says, meeting me in front of the door and pulling me in for a quick kiss.

I throw her a smirk before taking a step back. She's wearing a long-sleeved, black dress that hits about midthigh. Her dark hair is long and curly. She's beautiful. She blinks her blue eyes a couple of times and scrunches her nose. "You don't like what I'm wearing?"

"You're kidding, right?" I grab her wrist and pull her in close to me. "You are fucking beautiful." I nibble at her neck, and she giggles.

"Jack, stop. We have to go." Her tone is serious, but I know she could be easily persuaded.

We head out the door toward the rental, which we're driving since my Jeep was totaled in the accident. Luckily the guy who hit us has great insurance, and fortunate for him, he wasn't drunk, just an idiot who happened to exit onto the highway going in the wrong direction. It's also fortunate for him that he wasn't injured because it could have been so much worse for everyone involved.

We climb inside the small car and buckle up before I start the engine and back out of the driveway.

"Where are we going?" Jovie asks a few minutes later as she shifts in her seat, turning her body so she's facing me. "You just missed the turn to go to Stone's house." She's confused, and it's so damn cute.

The small car rolls to a stop at a traffic light. "Oh, yeah. I forgot to mention that I want to show you something first. Is that okay?" I glance over at her because I want to see the look on her face.

"Sure." She gives me an unsure smile but doesn't ask any questions.

About ten minutes later, we pull into the parking lot of the place I'd planned on bringing her to at midnight Christmas

Eve/Christmas Day morning, but fate had different plans for us, so instead we were on lockdown in a hospital room and she was dreaming about Piper. It hurts me to even think about how she must have felt dreaming about her sister. Even though there was an eight-year age difference between them, they were very close.

"Where are we?" she asks as the car rolls to a stop. She immediately takes off her seat belt and opens the door. "And why are we at the back of the building? This is kind of creepy, Jack. There's no one else around." She looks over her shoulder at me before getting out of the car.

"Babe, so many questions. Just give me a second and you'll understand everything."

"If you say so." She stands just inside the door of the car, giving me plenty of time to take in her beauty. My gaze travels down her petite frame and finally lands on her perfectly toned ass. She's so fucking beautiful. "Jack, what's taking you so long?"

Her question jars me out of my lustful gaze, and I hop out of the car, closing the door behind me. She meets me at the front of the vehicle, and I take her hand in mine. Without any lights on the backside of the building, it's a lot darker than I expected, so I hand her my phone and we use the light to find our way to the door on the right end of the building. Once the door is open and we step inside, I flip the light on.

"What is this place?" she asks as she surveys the small room.

"Hang on a second and I'll answer all of your questions," I tell her as I guide her down a wide hallway, flipping a couple light switches until we reach our destination—the open room located in the front of the building. As soon as the last light comes on, her mouth falls open. She takes a step back away from me and gasps while her eyes travel quickly around the room, taking in every square inch. "Oh my God, Jack. Is this...." Her gaze lands back on mine.

"Yes, it is," I answer as I reach for her hand. "This is what I've been doing. Every day when I got off work at Southern Stain, I came here and worked my ass off. I did this for us—for our future." I swore I wouldn't let my damn nerves get the best of me, but I don't think I'm going to have any control over it. My heart is racing, and I'm sweating. *Just fucking great.*

"What do you mean?" Her eyes are wide as she continues to look around the room.

I move my hands to her waist and turn her to face the counter that stretches across most of the lobby. "Mad Jack's," she says, reading the bright red cursive writing that graces the sign hanging above the entry to the hallway.

"So, what do you think?" I wrap my arms around her and pull her body into mine.

"I think you are going to do so good on your own. I'm so happy for you, Jack. You've worked so hard." Her voice cracks before she lets out an audible sigh. "This place is amazing. Your own tattoo studio. I have so many questions, but right now I just want to stand here with you and take it all in," she says proudly.

I turn her around to face me, and as I stare into those blue eyes, I remember the first time I met her. She was having a panic attack, and all I wanted to do was make it go away, but I was a dumbass guy who didn't have a clue about a girl like Jovie. Now, I'm still a dumbass guy who doesn't have a clue, but the difference between then and now is that I love this girl with every single inch of my heart.

"Jovie, Mad Jack's is our future. I can't do it without you." I suck in a deep breath and blow it out slowly. Every muscle in my body is twitching as I shove my hand in the front pocket of my jeans and pull out the small velvet box that holds the ring I've had for months.

Jovie gasps as her hand covers her mouth. Her eyes are glassy, and her face is flushed. *Come on, Jack, be a fucking man and do what you came here to do.* I slowly lower myself to one knee, open the box, and look up into her beautiful blue eyes. "Jovie, baby, will you do this thing called life with me? Will you marry me and love me forever?" I wobble slightly as I try to keep my balance.

She nods as the word "Yes" falls from her mouth.

"Yes," I repeat. She nods again as tears fall from her eyes. My gut is in knots, and I just want to put this ring on her finger, take her home, and spend the next week in bed making up for lost time.

I slide the one-carat, petite solitaire, platinum ring onto her finger, and luckily, it's a perfect fit. She grabs my wrist and I stand, pulling her into my arms.

"Thank you for loving me, Jack, and I'm sorry I ever doubted you." She wraps her arms around my waist and squeezes me tightly.

"Jovie, look at me." I tip her head back slightly until I can see her eyes. "I know why you doubted me, and it was my fault because I wanted this to be a surprise. I never told you where I was going or who I was with. Hell, I felt guilty as shit telling you Mr. Thomas was a client when he's really my banker. I went about this all wrong, but I love you. Only you. Always you."

The End

A NOTE FROM THE AUTHOR

Dear Reader,

I'm so happy you took the time to read Twisted Fate and Twisted Surprise. I loved Jack and Jovie so much in Twisted Fate and loved them even more in Twisted Surprise. These two will always hold a special place in my heart. Luckily the words flowed easily and Jack and Jovie got an even happier ever after. Thank you so much for taking this journey with me back to where I started and thank you for loving Jack and Jovie.

Cheers,

Emery xoxo

ACKNOWLEDGMENTS

There are so many people to thank for being a part of this book writing journey. It would've been impossible to do alone.

Taylor Roth: Thank you for being the BEST PA ever!! Without you none of the important stuff would ever get done. Many—Many—thanks for designing graphics (teasers, FB Banners, etc.), making sign up forms that somehow become organized spreadsheets, BETA reading and telling me the TRUTH, promoting everything I write, hanging out with me and the BABES, listening to me talk about absolutely nothing for longer than you probably want to, and for organizing EVERYTHING. I'm sure I left some stuff out, but I hope you know how much I appreciate you!!

Debra and Drue: You guys are absolutely incredible. I'm so impressed with the job you two do. Without you nothing would get done (including but not limited my newsletter, any and all social media posting, book formatting, organizing cover reveals and release day events). Thank you for your guidance through the PR part of this journey. Without the two of you I would have fallen on my face (many times). Thanks for your support—you two are great at what you do and I'm so happy to have y'all on my team. You two are the BEST!

Dawn Alexander: You are the best developmental editor. Seriously—you are. Your guidance while I was writing Twisted Surprise helped me to develop the very best story for Jack and Jovie. Thank you so much. I'm so happy to have you on my team.

C. Marie: Thank you for being so kind to always work me in at the last minute. Your editing skills are better than great. I truly appreciate you.

Julie Deaton: Thank you for always working with my crazy time schedule. I was early this time (something that NEVER happens). Yay! Thank you for being so amazing. I couldn't ask for a better proofreader to have on my team. Couldn't do it without you!

Virginia at Hot Tree Editing: Thank you for being the final set of eyes to read Jack and Jovie's story. Your proofreading skills are excellent.

To my husband: you are wonderful, but I guess you already knew that, huh? Thanks for putting up with my many hours locked away in my office or talking about this book to the point of making you want to go anywhere just to get away from the sound of my voice.

To my son: Thank you for being you. My absolute greatest accomplishment. I'm thankful every day that I'm your mom.

To my mom: Thank you for always believing in me and giving me the freedom to make my own decisions. Sometimes it took me the long way around to get to where I was supposed to be, but I always made it.

To my Dad: I miss you every day. You always supported me and believed in me. Thank you for being the best Dad ever!

Amy Queau: Thank you for designing the perfect cover for Twisted Surprise. You somehow can read my mind (every time). You are the BEST!

Max Ellis: Thank you for the perfect image of Drew for Twisted Surprise's cover. If I hadn't seen this cover image—there wouldn't have been a Twisted Surprise Christmas novella.

Drew Truckle: Thank you for being so kind and supportive—for promoting and sharing my books and for always being my Jack.

To every blogger, reader, author and friend who has shared my teasers and cover, or who has promoted my book—thank you —because without your support no one would know my books existed.

Emery Jacobs' Book Babes—Thank you for supporting me and waiting patiently for me to release books. You guys are the VERY BEST!!

To the readers—thank you for taking a chance on a new author. You guys are truly AMAZING! I really hope you loved Jack and Jovie's story as much as I loved writing it.

ABOUT THE AUTHOR

Emery grew up in Southern Arkansas and has lived most of her adult life in Northern Louisiana. She spends her days working as a Nurse Practitioner in rural health and her nights reading, writing, and occasionally sleeping.

She loves real life romance...lots of angst and heartbreak, but always a happy ending.

Stay up to date with Emery!
Website: http://www.emeryjacobs.com
Email: emeryjacobswrites@gmail.com
Facebook Reader Group: https://www.facebook.com/
groups/954199601323358
Sign up for Emery's Newsletter: http://eepurl.com/bPxj5f

Or Follow her on

facebook.com/emeryjacobsauthor

twitter.com/ejacobswrites

instagram.com/emery_jacobs

goodreads.com/emeryjacobsauthor

bookbub.com/authors/emery-jacobs

ALSO BY EMERY JACOBS

Made in the USA
Lexington, KY
15 November 2019

57140495R00061